SPIDER-MAN

CLONE GENESIS

Gerry Conway
Len Wein
Archie Goodwin
writers

Ross Andru
Gil Kane
pencilers

Frank Giacoia
Dave Hunt
John Romita
Mike Esposito
inkers

Artie Simek
Joe Rosen
Ray Holloway
John Costanza
Annette Kawecki
letterers

Stan Goldberg
Petra Goldberg
Linda Lessmann
Janice Cohen
George Roussos
Don Warfield
Glynis Wein
colorists

SPIDER-MAN ™ : CLONE GENESIS Originally published in magazine form a
AMAZING SPIDER-MAN #'s 141-151 and GIANT-SIZE SPIDER-MAN #5. Publishe
by Marvel Comics, 387 Park Avenue South, New York, New York 10016
Copyright © 1974, 1975, 1995 Marvel Entertainment Group, Inc. All rights
reserved. Spider-Man and all prominent characters appearing herein and the
distinctive names and likenesses thereof are trademarks of Marvel Entertainmen
Group, Inc. No part of this book may be printed or reproduced in any manne
without the written permission of the publisher. ISBN #0-7851-0158-6.
GST #R127032052. Printed in Canada. First Printing: June, 1995
10 9 8 7 6 5 4 3 2 1

Roy Thomas
Len Wein
Marv Wolfman
original series editors

Glenn Greenberg
assistant editor

Tom Brevoort
editor

Bob Budiansky
editor in chief

Dawn Geiger
designer

Roger Bonas
reproduction dept.

Special Thanks To:
Stan Lee
John Romita, Sr.
Roy Thomas

Who knew?

Twenty years after the fact, a storyline created to solve a perceived public relations problem spawns a dramatic new direction for Marvel's most famous hero...

I'll say it again: Who knew?

How it started was, I killed this girl named Gwen Stacy...

Uh, maybe I better explain.

Let's begin at the beginning:

Memories...

I started writing Spider-Man when I was nineteen, the first permanent writer to follow Stan Lee on the character he created. (Roy Thomas scripted a few fill-in issues the year before I took over the book, but that was intended only as a temporary gig.)

To say I was thrilled to get the assignment doesn't begin to describe how I felt. I'd been a fan of Stan's writing since I bought my first Marvel Comic— **Fantastic Four** #4—and I'd read and collected **Amazing Spider-Man** starting with issue #1. Taking over from Stan Lee (on **Spider-Man** as well as on **Thor**) was the fulfillment of a dream. I had no illusions about equaling the impact of Stan's work. I was just ecstatic to follow in his footsteps.

Little did I know that someday other writers would be following in mine...

My first year on **Spider-Man** was kind of an apprenticeship under Spidey's long-time artist, John Romita Sr. (John's name even got first billing in the credits over mine, a unique situation for an artist at that time, and still pretty rare these days.) John and I discussed storylines with Stan and Roy, and I pretty much followed their directions. (Though I did originate one storyline, introducing a new villain called Hammerhead.) After a year of this, John became Marvel's Art Director and handed the penciling chores over to Gil Kane, while remaining on the book as inker. When John left as penciler, my "apprenticeship" was over, and I assumed top billing in the credits as writer.

It was a heady moment for a twenty-year- old kid from Brooklyn and Queens. At that time, Marvel wasn't publishing half a dozen new stories a month about Spider-Man. We had **Amazing Spider-Man** and **Marvel Team-Up** (which, as a team-up book, didn't seem to count as part of the orthodox mythology). For all intents and purposes, I was the sole Spider-Man writer, the primary architect of Spider-Man's life story

—subject to supervision by Stan and Roy, of course. Mine was a great and terrible power.

And as we all know, with great power comes great responsibility...

So naturally, my first thought was, "Let's **kill** somebody!"

Not.

Let me set the record straight once and for all: killing Gwen Stacy was **not** my idea. I admit I thoug it was a good idea (and I still do, because in my hear know Mary Jane makes a much better foil for Peter Parker than Gwen Stacy ever could), but the first person to give voice to the idea wasn't me.

It was John Romita.

And Stan agreed.

John broached the notion during one of our last plotting sessions. We were talking about Marvel's tra dition of dramatic change. Our characters' lives weren't static (as were the lives of characters in other companies' books, at that time). New characters wer introduced, old characters moved on, relationships changed, couples got married and had children, teenage heroes graduated high school and went to co lege. People died. And when people died in a Marv Comic, they were dead, and they **stayed** dead.

We agreed that nothing really **dramatic** had happened in Peter Parker's life since the death of Gwen's father, Captain Stacy.

Well, said John (more or less), why don't we kill Gwen?

It was a lightbulb moment. I thought the idea wa terrific. Peter was a character born from tragedy— the early loss of his parents, his misfit status in high school, the preventable murder of his Uncle Ben— who ached with an overdeveloped sense of responsi bility. The thought that he'd have to endure and tri umph over a new tragedy, and one so **personal**, delighted me as a writer. Tragedy and pathos are meat and potatoes to a guy like me. I loved the dramatic possibilities.

And more: With Gwen gone, Peter and Mary Jane could become a couple. I'd been a fan of Mary Jane since the moment Peter first laid eyes on her (in one of the first Spider-Man stories John Romita drew, by the way). In my mind, theirs was a match made in writer's heaven.

It was perfect.

We took the idea to Stan.

He thought it was perfect too. Stan the writer

ew a great dramatic setup when he saw one. No
e in comics had ever killed off a major love interest.
is was a story that would be talked about for
onths. Maybe years.

But decades?

Who knew?

We did the story. Gwen died, as poignantly as
y character in the history of comics. The manner of
r death was totally in keeping with Stan's theme of
ower and responsibility. Spider-Man, after all, is a
aracter whose triumphs always have been tainted by
intended tragic consequences. The Spider-Man
hose self-interest indirectly caused the murder of his
cle Ben is the same Spider-Man whose cavalier
eroism inadvertently contributes to the death of Gwen
acy.

It was, to say the least, a public relations disaster.

Letters. We got letters.

Phone calls. We got phone calls.

Readers **hated** us.

They hated **me**.

They hated **Stan**.

Matters came to a head when Stan was
mbushed by hecklers during a college lecture a few
eeks after the issue was published. How could Stan
o it? the hecklers demanded. How could he kill off
wen Stacy? There were boos, hisses, catcalls, cries
r blood. The audience rose as one, demanding
evenge.

Stan—a sweet, gentle-tempered man who wants
nly to be loved—was caught off guard and tried to
xplain. "I didn't do it," he told them. "Gerry did."

What he meant, of course, was that I'd written the
ory, not him. He wasn't trying to evade responsibility
e was, after all, publisher and editor-in-chief).
aybe his memory of the circumstances was faulty, or
erhaps he said something more ambiguous. But the
udience interpreted what he said to mean that Stan
ad been oblivious to what was happening at the com-
any he ran, and thus a legend was born:

The legend is: Gerry Conway killed off Gwen
tacy while Stan Lee was out of town.

I don't think so.

Well, anyway. For whatever reason Stan decided
hat killing off Gwen was a mistake that had to be rec-
fied.

He told me he wanted her brought back.

I objected, pointing out that one of Marvel's hal-
owed traditions—if not our most hallowed tradition—

was Rule One:

When somebody dies in a Marvel Comic, they're
dead, and they **stay** dead.

Gwen was dead.

She'd been buried.

She had a tombstone.

We **couldn't** bring her back.

"You're bright guys," Stan told us (by "us" I mean
Roy Thomas and me). "Do something, but bring her
back."

Steve Gerber, a writer at Marvel at the time, and
an editor of a Marvel black-and-white horror magazine called **Tales of the Zombie**, offered to give
her a feature in the mag and call it "Graveyard
Gwen."

Nice idea, but not really what Stan had in mind.

I wracked my brains for months trying to figure
out what to do.

How could I bring Gwen Stacy back from the
dead without invalidating everything Marvel stood for?
Our readers had experienced real pain because of her
death. We couldn't cheapen their experience by saying Gwen never really died. Their pain had to be hon-
ored. How could I do that and still fulfill Stan's man-
date?

Gwen was dead, she was just a memory.

How do you resurrect a memory?

The more I thought about it the more I understood
that bringing Gwen back from the dead was a propo-
sition doomed to failure.

Finally I realized: **that** was my story.

*Bringing Gwen back from the dead was a propo-
sition doomed to failure..*

When you read these "clone" stories, keep in
mind the theme I was trying to express: memory is a
treacherous thing.

We have to honor our memories but not be ruled
by them. We dare not forget the past, but we mustn't
live in yesterday.

Interestingly, it seems to me this is the theme being
explored by the new "Spider-Man clone" stories.

How much do our memories matter?

How much do our memories make us who we
are?

It wasn't my intention, twenty years ago, to create
a classic. But it seems, in a modest way, that I did. It's
flattering and gratifying.

But I ask you, who knew?

Gerry Conway

WHEN WE NEXT PICK UP OUR HARRIED HERO, IT'S SEVERAL HOURS *AFTER* THE ABORTIVE SPIDER-MOBILE CAPER--

--WITH FEW--

--POSITIVE--

--RESULTS.

--AS AN EXHAUSTED *PETER PARKER* TRIES TO STAY *AWAKE* DURING A CLASS IN BIO-CHEMISTRY--

MISTER PARKER-- THIS IS A LECTURE HALL, *NOT* A REST CAMP.

MAY I SUGGEST THAT IN THE FUTURE--YOU DO YOUR SLEEPING *AT HOME?*

WHA--? HUH? *OH!* SORRY, PRO-FESSOR....!

THE CLASS ENDS. IN GROUPS OR SINGLY, THE STUDENTS LEAVE...ALL BUT *ONE*, A CERTAIN SOMNOLENT SCHOLAR WHO IS ASKED TO RE-MAIN *AFTER* THE OTHERS ARE GONE, FOR A FRIENDLY "CHAT"...

PETER, I MUST ADMIT-- I'M *APPALLED.*

BECAUSE OF YOUR MARKS LAST YEAR, YOU'VE HAD TO TAKE *BIO CHEM* 106 OVER THIS SEMESTER--

AND PETER-- YOUR *SECOND* CHANCE IS YOUR *LAST* CHANCE.

I *KNOW* THAT, PROFESSOR WARREN--AND I'M GRATEFUL YOU LET ME REGISTER TO TAKE THE COURSE *AGAIN.*

THEN *SHOW* THAT GRATI-TUDE, PETER. *SHAPE UP.*

YOU HAVE IMMENSE *POTENTIAL*-- MORE THAN ANY *OTHER* STUDENT I'VE EVER HAD.

PLEASE, DON'T *WASTE* THAT POTENTIAL...DON'T *BETRAY* MY FAITH IN YOU.

IF YOU HAVE ANY PROBLEM --ANY *DIFFICULTY*--KNOW THAT I'M ALWAYS *AVAIL-ABLE* TO YOU.

I'D LIKE TO THINK WE HAVE A *GOOD* RELA-TIONSHIP, PETER, AS TEACHER AND PUPIL--EVEN AS *FRIENDS.*

THANKS, PROFESSOR WARREN.

BELIEVE ME--I MEAN THAT.

PETER'S ANSWERING SMILE IS A *WISTFUL* ONE. AND AS HE SMILES, HIS MIND GOES BACK TO *ANOTHER* GIRL--ANOTHER WOMAN --HE'S KNOWN.

THAT GIRL IS DEAD.

AND HE WONDERS...

CAN *ANYONE* REPLACE GWEN STACY, THE WOMAN HE LOVED?

PETER DOESN'T KNOW.

HE JUST...

DOESN'T KNOW.

THE AUTUMN WIND LIFTS LEAVES ACROSS THE *CITY*, GUSTING THEM FROM ONE PART OF TOWN TO *ANOTHER.*

IF WE *FOLLOW* THEM ACROSS TOWN, THEY TAKE US *HERE*--TO A CERTAIN *PRIVATE CLUB*--

--WHERE ONE OF THE MEMBERS IS *EXTREMELY* FAMILIAR!

GOOD AFTERNOON, MR. JAMESON.

WOULD YOU LIKE YOUR *USUAL?*

A SNIFTER OF BRANDY FOR BOTH *MR. ROBERTSON* AND MYSELF, NORTON.

AND, NORTON--I'M EX-PECTING AN IMPORTANT *PHONE CALL.* WHEN IT COMES, PLEASE NOTIFY ME AT ONCE--I'LL BE IN THE *MAIN SALON.*

VERY GOOD, SIR.

*L*IFE CAN BE QUITE *ELEGANT,* REALLY--*IF* YOU'RE A WELL-KNOWN PUBLISHER OF A MAJOR DAILY *NEWSPAPER,* AND IF YOU'RE RICH ENOUGH TO PAY $5,000.00 A YEAR FOR CLUB *DUES,* AND IF YOU REALLY *CARE* ABOUT SUCH THINGS--

*L*IFE CAN BE QUITE ELEGANT, INDEED.

MR. JAMESON ...YOUR *PHONE CALL,* SIR.

PHONE CALL, JONAH?

JUST A SMALL *BUSINESS DEAL* I'VE BEEN WORKING ON, ROBERTSON.

NOW, IF YOU'LL *EXCUSE* ME...

YES?

YES, THIS IS *JAMESON.*

...I SEE. SO YOU'VE MADE *CONTACT,* HAVE YOU?

EXCELLENT. FINE. I'LL EXPECT ANOTHER REPORT *TOMORROW.*

WELL.

WELL, WELL.

ANYTHING *WRONG,* JONAH?

ON THE *CONTRARY,* ROBERTSON. FOR THE FIRST TIME IN MANY YEARS...

EVERYTHING IS JUST *FINE.*

SOME OF OUR *OTHER* CAST-MEMBERS MIGHT NOT FEEL AS *KINDLY* AS JONAH DOES TOWARD LIFE THIS EVENING...AND KNOWING PETER PARKER AS WE DO, WE'D GUESS THAT *ONE* OF THOSE DISGRUNTLED CAST-MEMBERS JUST MIGHT BE A CERTAIN WEB-SLINGING *SPIDER-MAN...*

FIVE O'CLOCK ALREADY-- AND I STILL HAVEN'T FIGURED OUT A WAY TO SALVAGE MY *SPIDER-MOBILE!*

I'D CHUCK THE WHOLE THING AND SIMPLY *FORGET* IT, IF I HADN'T MADE A DEAL WITH THOSE CLOWNS AT *CORONA MOTORS* TO BUILD THE STUPID THING* --

BUT AS IT IS, I DON'T HAVE A *CHOICE:* I'VE GOT TO GET THE S-M BACK-- *SOON!*

BACK IN MARVEL TALES #103, SPORTS-FANS. -- ROY.

17

FLANNNGGG!

AFTER: PETER! OH, DEAR-- YOUR HANDS! HOW DID YOU HURT YOUR HANDS?

WOULD YOU BELIEVE I CAUGHT THEM IN A DOOR LEAVING SCHOOL?

FOR HEAVEN'S SAKE, PARKER-- BE SERIOUS.

YOU LOOK LIKE YOU'VE BEEN WORKED OVER BY A FOOTBALL TEAM.

MAYBE WE SHOULD CALL MR. ROBERTSON, NED.

HE COULD FIND A DOCTOR, AND--

DON'T BOTHER, BETTY. IT MIGHT CAUSE THE DAILY BUGLE A LITTLE MONEY--

AND I WOULDN'T WANT TO GET JONAH JAMESON ALL UPSET.

WILL YOU TELL US WHAT HAPPENED, PETER?

WHAT'S TO TELL? I GOT MIXED UP IN A BRAWL BETWEEN SPIDER-MAN AND MYSTERIO--MY HANDS ARE A LITTLE CUT-UP, THAT'S ALL.

APPARENTLY MYSTERIO'S ESCAPED FROM JAIL-- AND HE'S BACK IN TOWN, CARRYING A KING-SIZE GRUDGE FOR OUR FAVORITE WEB-SLINGER.

MYSTERIO? ARE YOU SURE?

A MISTAKE LIKE THAT'S PRETTY HARD TO MAKE, NED.

BUT YOU MUST HAVE MADE A MISTAKE, PETER... EITHER THAT, OR YOU SAW A GHOST.

MYSTERIO DIED IN PRISON ALMOST A YEAR AGO!

THEN-- IT'S FINALLY HAPPENED! I'M CRACKING UP--

PETER PARKER IS-- INSANE!

25

OUCH.

I SHOULDN'T HAVE PUT MY *WEIGHT* ON MY HAND LIKE THAT.

MY FINGERS ARE STILL TOO *TENDER*--

--AND THEY *SHOULD* BE, EVEN *BANDAGED.*

I'M LUCKY I DIDN'T *FRACTURE* THEM.

AFTER ALL, WHEN YOU USE A BRICK WALL FOR A *PUNCHING BAG*--

--*SOMETHING'S* GOT TO GIVE-- AND IT PROBABLY *WON'T* BE THE *WALL.*

I DON'T KNOW WHICH BOTHERS ME *MORE*-- THE FACT I THOUGHT I SAW MY OLD *ENEMIES* APPEARING THROUGH THAT WALL--

--OR THE FACT I ALMOST SMASHED MY KNUCKLES *FIGHTING* THEM!

YOU HAVE TO BE PRETTY *SLOW* NOT TO-- *HUH*?

FOOTSTEPS-- UP ON TOP OF THE *PIER.*

AND SOMETHING TELLS ME IT'S...

MYSTERIO!

YOU KNOW, FRIEND-- FOR A *GHOST*, YOU SURE GET *AROUND.*

THE MIST-ENSHROUDED FIGURE MAKES NO *ANSWER*--

--UNTIL, AT LAST, HE TURNS AND *GOES AWAY.*

NO PARKING
THIS SIDE OF SIGN
MON.-TUES 9 AM

AND THIS IS WHERE HE GOES AWAY *TO:* HIS NEW APARTMENT IN MANHATTAN'S *CHELSEA DISTRICT,* ON THE LOWER WEST SIDE--

--WHERE WE FIND HIM A LITTLE LATER, MAKING USE OF HIS RECENTLY-INSTALLED *TELEPHONE* TO CALL A CERTAIN DOTING *AUNT* OF HIS...

AUNT MAY MUST BE WORRIED *SICK* ABOUT ME-- AND WHAT *ELSE* IS NEW?

EVER SINCE I MOVED OUT OF OUR HOUSE IN *FOREST HILLS,* SHE'S BEEN SURE I'D FALL INTO THE HANDS OF *GANGSTERS*--

--OR *WORSE.*

BRANNGG

PETER! MY, THIS *IS* A SURPRISE!

I WAS JUST *THINKING* ABOUT YOU, YOU *DARLING* BOY...

DO YOU LIKE YOUR NEW *APARTMENT?*

IT'S *SWELL,* AUNT MAY. IT'D BE EVEN *BETTER* IF I HAD ANY *FURNITURE.*

EXCUSE ME A SECOND-- *MARY JANE* JUST WALKED IN.

TAKE A *SEAT,* MJ.

WHAT? OH, I'LL DIG UP SOME BEDS AND CHAIRS *SOME-WHERE...* THAT'S THE *LEAST* OF MY PROBLEMS.

WHAT? DID I SAY *PROBLEMS?*

SORRY. SLIP OF THE *TONGUE.*

EVERYTHING'S *FINE.* SURE, I'M SURE.

LISTEN, I ONLY CALLED TO LET YOU KNOW I'M *OKAY*, AUNT MAY.

NO, NOTHING'S *WRONG*, SWEETHEART...

...I'VE BEEN *EATING* REGULARLY, WEARING WARM CLOTHES...USING UMBRELLAS WHEN IT RAINS... EVERYTHING YOU ALWAYS *TOLD* ME TO--

KINGPIN!

MARY JANE--

LOOK OUT!

SPRANNGG!

HE'S--HE'S *GONE*--

--VANISHED--JUST LIKE--*MYSTERIO*--!

OF COURSE! MYSTERIO'S BEHIND THIS-- SOMEHOW, HE--

PETEY, WHAT--

ARE YOU *OKAY*?

PETER! PETER, WHAT HAPPENED?

HEAVEN ABOVE, *PETER--!*

AH...*AUNT MAY?* PETER HERE. I'M *SORRY* ABOUT THAT... UH...IT WAS A *MISTAKE.*

A MISTAKE? PETER, YOU SHOULDN'T *DO* SUCH THINGS!

YES, I *KNOW* HOW UPSET YOU ARE, AUNT MAY-- AND AGAIN, I'M *REALLY* SORRY.

I--UH-- CAN'T TALK NOW, BUT I'LL EXPLAIN ALL ABOUT IT *LATER.*

PLEASE DON'T *WORRY,* THOUGH-- OKAY?

OKAY.

TIGER, YOUR AUNT ISN'T THE *ONLY* LADY WORRIED ABOUT YOU.

THE WAY YOU *LOOKED* AT ME--

SAY, MAN-- WHAT'S GOING *ON* IN HERE?

OH-- *NI,* GLORIA.

NELLO, MRS. MUGGINS.

DON'T YOU HELLO *ME,* MR. PARKER.

THIS IS AN APARTMENT *BUILDING--* NOT A *BOXING RING.*

IF YOU'RE THE SORT OF MAN WHO LIKES TO THROW THINGS *AROUND--*

--WELL, THEN YOU CAN THROW *YOURSELF* RIGHT *OUT* OF HERE!

YOU MEAN-- THAT--AH-- *PHONE* I DROPPED?

THAT WAS AN *ACCIDENT,* MRS. MUGGINS-- IT WON'T HAPPEN *AGAIN.*

HAH! THAT'S WHAT MY *BARNEY* ALWAYS SAYS WHEN HE'S FEELIN' A LITTLE *RESTLESS.*

I'LL LET IT GO *THIS* TIME--

--BUT *WATCH* YOURSELF, SONNY. I'M *WARNING* YOU.

YOU SURE KNOW HOW TO MAKE *FRIENDS,* PETER-BOY, AND SPEAKING OF FRIENDS-- WHO'S YOUR *FRIEND?*

OH, GLORY. THIS IS *MARY JANE WATSON.* WE GO *WAY BACK.*

MJ, THIS IS *GLORY GRANT.*

GLORY, CUTE NAME.

MJ, SPIFFY TAG.

PETER, MY MAN, I JUST CAME BY TO TELL YOU ABOUT A *PARTY* I'M RIGGING FOR NEXT WEEKEND.

WHY DON'T YOU *SHOW* FOR IT, HMM?

"PETER, MY MAN"? HOW LONG HAVE YOU *KNOWN* EACH OTHER, TIGER?

AS A MATTER OF FACT, MJ--

--I'M *NOT SURE.*

WE'LL HAVE OURSELVES A REAL *TIME.*

SLAM!

Panel 1:
--AND SO DOES MY FAVORITE *GIRL FRIDAY*.

HEH-HEH, I MEAN *PERSON* FRIDAY, MS. BRANT.

RUN ALONG, YOU TWO. *RUN ALONG.*

Panel 2:
MR. ROBERTSON-- DO YOU GET THE FEELING YOU'VE BEEN *TAKEN* SOMEHOW?

BETTY, WITH JONAH-- I *ALWAYS* FEEL LIKE I'VE BEEN TAKEN.

BUT *THIS*-- WELL, TO PUT IT *MILDLY*--

THE MAN MUST BE *SICK*.

Panel 3:
IS ANYTHING *WRONG*, MR. ROBERTSON?

PARKER! I'VE BEEN TRYING TO GET *AHOLD* OF YOU, SON.

Panel 4:
MIND IF WE HAVE A *TALK*? IT'S ABOUT THIS *MYSTERIO* THING...

YES, SHE *DID*, PETER...

MARY JANE, I HOPE YOU DON'T *MIND*--

I GUESS BETTY MUST HAVE TOLD YOU ABOUT *LAST NIGHT*, HUH?*

COFFEE-MAT

BUT DO YOU REMEMBER A CONVERSATION YOU AND I HAD AT MY *CHRISTMAS PARTY* LAST YEAR?

*LAST ISSUE.--LEN.

Panel 5:
ABOUT *PETEY*-- AND MY *FEELINGS* FOR HIM? SURE I REMEMBER, BETTY.

I TOLD YOU THEN, I DIDN'T KNOW IF I *WANTED* TO FEEL SERIOUS ABOUT PETE-- AND I *MEANT* THAT-- THEN.

I GUESS YOU COULD SAY, MAYBE THINGS HAVE *CHANGED*...

Panel 6:
EARLIER THIS EVENING, PETE STARTED ACTING *STRANGE*-- AND IT *FRIGHTENED* ME A LITTLE.

I FELT AS THOUGH SOMEONE I-- OH, *HI*, NED.

'LO, MJ. BETTY TELL YOU THE *NEWS*?

"NEWS"--?

Panel 7:
WELL-- WE'VE BEEN KEEPING IT A *SECRET*, AND I DIDN'T WANT TO *TELL* YOU-- WHILE WE WERE TALKING ABOUT YOU AND PETER...

BUT NED AND I-- WE'VE FINALLY SET THE *DATE*.

YOU MEAN-- TO GET *MARRIED*?

Panel 8:
FAR *OUT*.

THAT'S SIMPLY THE MOST--

FAR *OUT*.

I CAN'T TELL YOU HOW--

WOW.

35

YOU'VE **GOT** TO TELL PETEY!

HEY, TIGER-- GUESS WHO'S GONNA BE A **BLUSHIN'** BRIDE?

STUMBLING EXPLANATIONS ARE MADE, AND WHEN THE EXPLAINING IS **DONE**...

I CAN'T WISH YOU ENOUGH HAPPINESS, BETTY.

ALL **I** CAN SAY, NED, IS--

--IT'S ABOUT **TIME**.

LATER...

FUNNY...

WHAT'S FUNNY, BLUE-EYES?

BETTY BRANT WAS THE FIRST GIRL I EVER FELL IN LOVE WITH.

THE **FIRST**, M.J.

THERE WAS A TIME WHEN I HATED NED LEEDS' **GUTS**.

NOW-- I LIKE HIM. TIMES CHANGE, LOVES CHANGE. YOU CAN NEVER--

OUTSIDE THE **ELEVATOR**-- WALKING THROUGH THE **LOBBY**--

IT'S **HER!**

MARY JANE WATSON OPENS HER MOUTH IN **AMAZEMENT**--

--BUT, BEFORE SHE CAN **SPEAK**--

--PETER IS OUT- SIDE, STARING AT A WALKING **DREAM**--

--THAT IS ALSO PART PAINFUL **NIGHTMARE**.

IT'S A **TRICK**-- --ANOTHER OF MYSTERIO'S **ILLUSIONS**--!

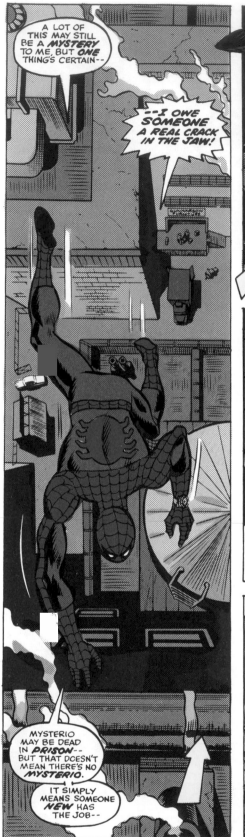

A LOT OF THIS MAY STILL BE A *MYSTERY* TO ME, BUT *ONE* THING'S CERTAIN--

--*I* OWE *SOMEONE* A REAL CRACK IN THE JAW!

MYSTERIO MAY BE DEAD IN *PRISON*-- BUT THAT DOESN'T MEAN THERE'S NO *MYSTERIO.*

IT SIMPLY MEANS SOMEONE *NEW* HAS THE JOB--

--AND *WHOEVER* HE IS, I'M GOING TO *FIND* HIM--AND WHEN I DO, USING THIS HANDY *TRACKING DEVICE*--

--HE'S GOING TO *RUE* THE DAY HE WAS *BORN!*

IT'S TOO BAD FOR *HIM* I DISCOVERED THE *IMAGE-INDUCER* HE PLANTED ON MY COSTUME DURING OUR *DOCK-FIGHT.*

I WAS BEGINNING TO THINK I WAS *IMAGINING* THINGS-- SEEING *KINGPIN* IN MY APARTMENT, THEN THAT *OTHER* ILLUSION--

--BUT *NO,* IT'S JUST THIS GIZMO ON MY *CHEST.*

MYSTERIO HAS BEEN *TRANSMITTING* PICTURES TO THE GIZMO, AND IT'S BEEN *PROJECTING* THEM ONTO THE AIR IN *FRONT* OF ME.

LIKE THAT IMAGE OF THE *MINDWORM*--

--AN *ILLUSION* --A *TRICK!*

THAT AGONIZING THOUGHT WELL IN MIND, SPIDER-MAN CONTINUES ON TO HIS DESTINATION...THE DAILY BUGLE BUILDING, AND THE OFFICE OF ITS HOT-TEMPERED PUBLISHER...

AW. NOBODY'S HOME.

EVER SINCE MYSTERIO WENT OFF TO JAIL LAST WEEK, I'VE HAD THE FEELING JONAH JAMESON KNEW MORE ABOUT WHAT HAPPENED THAN HE LET ON.

I'VE BEEN SO BUSY WITH COLLEGE, I HAVEN'T HAD A CHANCE TO ASK HIM ABOUT IT BEFORE--

--AND NOW, IT SEEMS I'VE MISSED MY CHANCE.

J.J.J.'S "IN AND OUT" FILE IS USUALLY PILED WITH PAPERS. NOW IT'S EMPTY. WHY?

I GUESS THERE'S ONLY ONE ANSWER: JAMESON ISN'T HERE--AND HASN'T BEEN FOR SOME TIME!

THE QUESTION NOW BECOMES--WHERE IS HE AND HOW LONG IS HE GOING TO BE GONE?

JONAH'S SECRETARY WOULDN'T TELL SPIDER-MAN--

--BUT SHE'LL PROBABLY TELL PETER PARKER.

AFTER ALL, BETTY AND I USED TO GO TOGETHER--

--EVEN IF IT DOES SEEM LIKE AN ETERNITY AGO.

HELLO THERE, PRETTY LADY. HOW GOES THE PAPER BIZ?

PETER!

49

--IT *DOES* HAVE A FEW PLACES THAT ARE ALMOST *PRIVATE:*

ATTENTION. ATTENTION. FLIGHT 907 TO PARIS, FRANCE, VIA LONDON IS NOW BOARD-ING AT GATE 5.

ATTENTION. ATTENTION. FLIGHT 907--

LOOK, TIGER-- I WANT YOU TO TAKE REAL GOOD *CARE* OF YOURSELF, OKAY?

SURE THING, MARY JANE --IF YOU'LL ANSWER ONE *QUES-TION* FOR ME BEFORE I LEAVE.

ONE QUESTION....?

WHY DO YOU ALWAYS CALL ME *TIGER?*

WHY DO I--? OH, PETEY-- I CALL YOU TIGER 'CAUSE YOU'RE *NOT!*

NOW, *C'MERE,* TIGER, AND KISS M-- MMMMMMM.

*S*OMETHING HAPPENS.

*M*AYBE *THIS* IS THE MOMENT EACH HAS BEEN *WAITING* FOR.

*M*AYBE NOW, WHEN THEY ARE ABOUT TO *SEPARATE*--SOME-THING FINALLY BRINGS THEM *TOGETHER.*

*W*HATEVER THE REASON--

--SOMETHING HAPPENS--

50

--AND NEITHER HE NOR SHE WILL EVER BE THE *SAME*.

WOW.

WHY DIDN'T YOU EVER *TELL* ME YOU COULD *KISS*?

I MEAN... WOW.

MJ... I...

WHY, PETER-- ARE YOU *BLUSHING* OR IS THAT *ACNE*?

AM I WHAT? IS IT *WHAT*--?

HA HA HA HA HA

AND PETER PARKER *LAUGHS*.

COME ALONG, PETER. THAT'S OUR *PLANE* BOARDING UP AHEAD.

WHATEVER YOU SAY, MR. ROBERTSON. MJ--

--WELL-- I'LL BE *BACK*.

AND I'LL BE *WAITING*--

TIGER.

53

NO DOUBT YOU'RE ASKING YOURSELF: WHAT *EXACTLY* IS GOING ON HERE?

HAVE PATIENCE, AND GIVE US A FEW MORE PAGES OF YOUR TIME, AND WE'LL EXPLAIN...*EXACTLY*...

IF I DIDN'T *KNOW* BETTER--

--I'D BEGIN TO BELIEVE ROBBIE WAS LEADING ME ON A *WILD GOOSE CHASE!*

BUT THAT'S FLAT-OUT *IMPOSSIBLE.*

NOT ONLY IS HE UNAWARE THAT *SPIDER-MAN* IS IN FRANCE...

...HE'S *GOT* TO BE UNAWARE THAT I'M *FOLLOWING* HIM.

NO, MORE LIKELY IT'S A *PLAN.*

NOT *HIS* PLAN--THE KIDNAPPERS'.

THEY TOLD HIM TO HAVE HIS CAB *DRIVE AROUND* LIKE THAT--

--TO *LOSE* ANYONE WHO MIGHT TRY TO TRAIL ROBBIE AND CATCH THE *CROOKS.*

"*ORDINARILY,* IT WOULD HAVE *SUCCEEDED,* TOO--BUT NOT WHEN THE TRAILER IS YOUR FRIENDLY-NEIGHBORHOOD--*HUH?*

"*THAT VOICE* CALLING TO ROBBIE FROM UNDER THE BRIDGE--

MONSIEUR ROBERTSON...

--THEN TO BE BEATEN UP *MYSELF,* BY THEIR BOSS, THE MAN CALLED *CYCLONE!*

WHEN THE *LIGHTS* CAME ON AGAIN, CYCLONE AND HIS BUDDIES WERE *GONE*--AND SO WAS *ROBBIE.*

THOM!

WHICH LEAVES ME WITH A MILLION DOLLARS IN NEGOTIABLE BONDS IN OUR *HOTEL*--

--A SOMEWHAT SWEATY *SPIDER-SUIT*--

--AND A KINGSIZE CONTINENTAL *HEADACHE!*

FACE IT, HERO: THINGS HAVEN'T BEEN GOING YOUR WAY, LATELY.

FIRST YOU DUMP YOUR *SPIDER-MOBILE* IN THE HUDSON RIVER BACK IN NEW YORK--

--THEN YOU RUN INTO A NEW VERSION OF *MYSTERIO*--WITH A WHOLE SET OF ATTENDANT *ILLUSIONS*--!

--AND AS IF THAT WEREN'T *ENOUGH*--

--SOMETHING FINALLY *CLICKS* BETWEEN YOU AND *MARY JANE*--

--JUST AS YOU'RE LEAVING NEW YORK FOR *THIS* DISASTER! WITH YOUR KIND OF LUCK YOU'LL PROBABLY BE STUCK WITH THE BILL FOR THIS *HOTEL*--!

MONSIEUR PARKER--?

NOW WHAT?

YES? I MEAN-- *OUI?*

OUTSIDE, THE STREETS OF PARIS ARE PALE IN THE LIGHT OF EARLY *DAWN.* A CLINGING FOG HANGS OVER THE CITY, LENDING A *MUTED* QUALITY TO THE LONELY SOUNDS OF PETER'S FOOTSTEPS AS HE MOVES DOWN THE NARROW DESERTED STREET...

SENS UNIQUE

ARRÊTE

PARISIANS DON'T BELIEVE IN RISING EARLY ON A *SATURDAY.* THERE'S SOMETHING *INDECENT* ABOUT THE IDEA.

THUS, PETER FINDS HIMSELF *ALONE* WITH HIS THOUGHTS, WANDERING THE BYWAYS AND ALLEYS OF THIS STRANGELY PROVINCIAL METROPOLIS--

--WANDERING, UNTIL HE FINDS HIMSELF *HERE:*

A *HARDWARE* STORE. I HADN'T REALLY *THOUGHT* ABOUT IT-- BUT MAYBE THERE'S A WAY TO *DEFEAT* THE CYCLONE.

AND MAYBE I CAN FIND WHAT I *NEED*-- IN A PLACE LIKE THIS!

A MOMENT AGO, PETER PARKER WAS *DEPRESSED,* LISTLESS AND MORE THAN USUALLY GLOOMY.

NOW HE'S PRACTICALLY *EXPLODING* WITH EAGERNESS.

TALKING QUICKLY, HE EXPLAINS TO THE BILINGUAL SHOPKEEPER WHAT HE WANTS--

--AND, AFTER COMPLETING THE NECESSARY FISCAL TRANSACTIONS, TAKES *POSSESSION* OF THE PURCHASED EQUIPMENT, SETS IT ON A TROLLEY--

--AND VANISHES INTO THE MORNING *MIST*--

--HEADING, IT MIGHT BE WELL TO NOTE, TOWARD THE *CATHEDRAL OF NOTRE DAME!*

THE DAY PASSES WITH ALMOST UNENDURABLE **SLOWNESS.** AFTER COMPLETING HIS ARRANGEMENTS AT NOTRE DAME, PETER CHANGES TO HIS WEB-SLINGING **ALTER-EGO,** FOR SOME TENSION-RELIEVING **ACTION** DURING THE REMAINDER OF THIS LONG, CHILLY DAY...

FINALLY, HAVING COVERED MOST OF PARIS THREE TIMES **OVER,** SPIDEY TURNS AT LAST TOWARD THE ISLAND SET IN THE CENTER OF THE **SEINE RIVER**--

--THE ISLAND ON WHICH SITS THE CENTURIES-OLD CATHEDRAL THAT IS HIS **DESTINATION.**

NOW I KNOW HOW **QUASIMODO** FELT, LOOKING AT THOSE **GARGOYLES.**

THERE'S SOMETHING **PEACEFUL** ABOUT THOSE STONE STATUES.

THEY DON'T HAVE TO **DEAL** WITH LIFE-- WHILE **I DO.**

SOME DAYS I ALMOST WISH THE WORLD WOULD **GO AWAY,** SO I WOULDN'T HAVE TO **WORRY** ABOUT THINGS.

BUT IF IT **DID**-- IF EVERYTHING THAT BOTHERED ME **VANISHED**--

--THEN ALL THE **GOOD** THINGS WOULD VANISH **TOO**--

--INCLUDING GOOD THINGS LIKE *MARY JANE!*

SO MUCH FOR STOPPING THE WORLD AND *GETTING OFF.*

I GUESS MY TROUBLES ARE HERE TO *STAY.*

MEANWHILE, *INSIDE* THE CATHEDRAL--

I TRUST YOU ARE *COMFORTABLE,* MON AMI ?

THE TRIP HERE DID NOT OVERLY *DISCOMMODE* YOU, NO ?

LISTEN, YOU--!

I'M AN *AMERICAN CITIZEN,* AND YOU CAN'T JUST KIDNAP--

AHH, BUT I *CAN,* MONSIEUR JAMESON. I *HAVE.*

THE PROBLEM WITH YOU AMERICANS IS--YOU CANNOT *UNDERSTAND* YOUR OWN *VULNERABILITY.*

WE EUROPEANS, HOWEVER-- WE HAVE *EXPERIENCED* DEFEAT ON A VERY PERSONAL LEVEL. IT HAS MADE US *STRONG.*

YOU AMERICANS-- ARE *WEAK.*

THAT'S WHY YOU HAD TO USE THAT *CYCLONE* GADGET, EH ?

BECAUSE YOU'RE SO *STRONG--?*

THIS?

MONSIEUR, THIS DEVICE COULD HAVE BEEN THE *WORLD'S* BUT YOUR COUNTRY *REFUSED* IT--

"--AND REJECTED ME."

"I WAS A N.A.T.O. ENGINEER, AND I DEVELOPED *THE CYCLONE* AS A WEAPON OF *WAR*--

"--BUT WAS TOLD THAT N.A.T.O. DID NOT *REQUIRE* MY INVENTION, SINCE ALL EXOTIC WEAPONRY WOULD BE PURCHASED ONLY FROM *AMERICA.*"

"I WAS *ALSO* TOLD--"

"--N.A.T.O. DID NOT NEED ME."

SO *THAT'S* IT.

YOU'RE BLAMING *AMERICA* --AND *AMERICANS* --BECAUSE OF YOUR OWN *INCOMPETENCE!*

YOU'RE *CRAZY!*

A FEW MOMENTS LATER, A SEETHING PETER PARKER ARRIVES ON A SNOW-COVERED *ROOFTOP*, WHERE...

MAN, DOES THAT MAKE ME *MAD*. NOT JUST FOR WHAT SEEING "GWEN" DID TO *ME*--

--BUT FOR WHAT IT'S PROBABLY DONE TO *AUNT MAY*!

ANNA WATSON SAID AUNT MAY WAS IN THE *HOSPITAL*-- AND I CAN GUESS *WHY*.

I'D BETTER GET TO HER AS QUICKLY AS I *CAN*--

--AND THAT MEANS TRAVELING *SPIDER-MAN STYLE!*

POOR AUNT MAY MUST THINK SHE'S GOING *INSANE*-- LIKE *I* ALMOST THOUGHT--AND THE SHOCK MUST HAVE BROUGHT ON HER OLD *HEART TROUBLE!*

WELL, THAT'S JUST *ONE MORE THING* THE MYSTERY MAN BEHIND GWEN'S RESURRECTION IS GOING TO *PAY* FOR--

--WHICH IS WHY I'M GLAD MY *WEB-SHOOTERS* ARE STILL IN TIP-TOP SHAPE!

BECAUSE, WHEN I FIND HIM--AND I *WILL*--I'M GOING TO TRUSS THAT CLOWN UP--

--AND--

--AND--

HECK, I DON'T KNOW *WHAT* I'M GOING TO DO.

THERE'S A NOTE OF PAINED **RESIGNATION** IN OUR HAPLESS HERO'S VOICE; A TONE WHICH WOULD HAVE **SHOCKED** HIM ONLY A FEW **HOURS** AGO.

A MAN CAN TAKE ONLY **SO MUCH** FROM THE WORLD BEFORE HE GETS A LITTLE **PUNCH-DRUNK.** ONE DAY, THE BURDEN HE HAS TO BEAR GETS JUST A BIT **TOO HEAVY**--

--AND THE DELICATE STRUCTURE OF HIS EMOTIONS COMES TUMBLING **DOWN**--

--AND ALL AT ONCE, HE CEASES TO **CARE.**

SO, WHILE OUR WORLD-WEARY PROTAGONIST JOURNEYS CROSS-TOWN TO THE HOSPITAL WHERE HIS **AUNT MAY** IS KEPT IN INTENSIVE CARE, WE'LL TAKE OUR LEAVE, AND LOOK **ELSEWHERE** FOR OUR ENTERTAINMENT--

PRISON BUS

SPECIFICALLY, WE'LL LOOK **HERE:** A FEDERAL PENITENTIARY IN **NEW JERSEY,** WHERE A CERTAIN INMATE IS IN THE PROCESS OF BEING PROCESSED **OUT.**

TAKE A **CLOSE LOOK,** READER. YOU MIGHT **RECOGNIZE** THE MAN...

FOR WE HAVE, AFTER ALL, SEEN HIM **BEFORE**...

YOU WERE A **MODEL PRISONER,** GARGAN. IF YOU DON'T MIND--

--I'D LIKE TO SHAKE YOUR **HAND.**

SAVE IT FOR **SUNDAY SCHOOL,** PAL. I'VE SERVED MY **TIME.**

JUST LET ME **OUT.**

AND SO, MOMENTS LATER, A FAMILIAR *RED-AND-BLUE FIGURE* SWOOPS ACROSS THE TWILIGHT SKY--

--CONSUMED BY PASSIONS TOO *COMPLEX* FOR US TO QUICKLY UNDERSTAND--

--THOUGH UNDERSTAND THEM WE *WILL*--

--AT A *LATER* TIME.

FOR NOW, LET'S *TURN AWAY* FROM MANHATTAN'S *GRAMERCY PARK,* WHERE GWEN STACY IS BOARDING WITH *BETTY BRANT*--

--AND *LOOK HERE* FOR OUR STORY: A QUIET COUNTRY HOME IN MONTICELLO, NEW YORK--

--WHERE A CERTAIN *SCORPION* IS PREPARING TO MAKE A *BID*--

--FOR *POWER.*

HOW IN THE-- *HUNH?*

THE *SCORPION?* WHAT'RE YOU DOIN' *HERE?* DON'TYA KNOW WHO *OWNS* THIS PLACE?

AARRRAFFARRofe

I SURE *DO,* BUSTER--

GIVE THE MAN A *CIGAR*...

CHA-RING!

87th PRECINCT, MEYER SPEAKING. **WHO**? OH YEAH? IF YOU'RE **SPIDER-MAN**, THEN I'M--

HUNH? YOU'VE FOUND **WHAT**--?

THE LOOT FROM YESTERDAY'S **HOLD UP**--THE ONE PULLED BY THE SCORPION, REMEMBER?

NEWSFLASH: IT'S IN HIS **HOTEL ROOM** UP IN **WASHINGTON HEIGHTS.**

DON'T **MENTION** IT, OFFICER--

"--I'M ALWAYS HAPPY TO HELP THE **POLICE**."

SO MUCH FOR FINDING THE STOLEN MONEY.

NOW HOW DO I FIND **THE SCORPION**?

AFTER PONDERING SAID QUESTION FOR ALMOST AN **HOUR**, OUR ERSTWHILE HERO MOMENTARILY **ABANDONS** HIS SEARCH TO VISIT A CERTAIN ELDERLY **RELATIVE** STAYING IN A MIDTOWN HOSPITAL...THE IMMORTAL OLD WOMAN KNOWN AS **AUNT MAY**...

YOU SHOULDN'T CONCERN YOURSELF ABOUT **ME**, PETER DEAR. THE DOCTOR SAYS I'LL BE **FINE**.

IT WAS SIMPLY THE **SHOCK** OF SEEING GWEN AGAIN--AFTER THOSE RUMORS OF HER **DEATH**--

THEY WEREN'T **RUMORS**, AUNT MAY--

--BUT HOW CAN I **EXPLAIN** THAT, WHEN I DON'T QUITE BELIEVE IT **MYSELF**?

BECAUSE SHE CAN'T ACCEPT WHAT SHE **SAW**, AUNT MAY HAS CREATED A **FANTASY**--

--IN WHICH GWEN **HASN'T** RETURNED FROM THE DEAD, BUT SHE NEVER REALLY **DIED**!

MAYBE **I** SHOULD--HUH?

KRASH!

PETER! THAT **NOISE** FROM BEYOND THE **CURTAIN**! WHAT--?

105

107

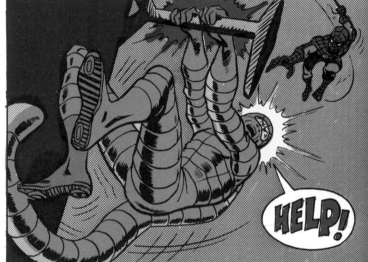

FOR SOME REASON I'VE NEVER *UNDERSTOOD*, JONAH ALWAYS PAYS HIS *OFFICE* PEOPLE BETTER THAN HIS *REPORTERS*.

OR, IN *MY* CASE--HIS *PHOTOGRAPHERS*.

I HAVE *ENOUGH* PROBLEMS WITH MY LIFE WITHOUT WORRYING ABOUT BETTY BRANT'S *PAYCHECK*.

WELL... HERE'S HER *APARTMENT*...

I GUESS IT'S A CASE OF *"OUT OF SIGHT, OUT OF MIND."*

BECAUSE I DON'T WORK AT THE BUGLE NINE-TO-FIVE, JAMESON JUST DOESN'T *THINK* ABOUT ME.

EITHER THAT, OR HE FIGURES HE CAN *AVOID* ME IF NECESSARY--

I MIGHT AS WELL GET THIS *OVER* WITH.

BR
NG!

--WHILE HE *CAN'T* AVOID HIS REGULAR *EMPLOYEES.*

ANYWAY WHO *CARES*

YES? WHO *IS* IT...?

IT'S *ME*, GWEN-- PETER.

I-I CAN'T *TALK* TO YOU, PETER-- I-I NEED TIME TO *THINK*--

GWEN... ARE YOU *ALL RIGHT?*

10-C

STREET SCENE: HOMEWARD FLIES THE CONQUERING HERO.

WELL, ALMOST.

MORE THAN A LITTLE WEARY AFTER HIS ADVENTURE WITH THE MAN-THING IN THE FLORIDA EVERGLADES*, OUR FRIENDLY NEIGHBOR-HOOD WEB-SPINNER HAS HITCHED A RIDE FROM THE AIRPORT TO THE CITY--

*SEE GIANT-SIZE SPIDER-MAN #5.--LEN.

--AND NOW, THAT RIDE IS AT AN END.

WHICH MEANS, OF COURSE--

--OUR STORY'S JUST BEGINNING:

HELLO THERE, DAILY BUGLE.

GUESS WHO'S BACK FROM THE SWAMP-LAND?

THAT'S RIGHT, BUGLE-- ME, YOUR EVER-LOVIN' STAR PHOTOGRAPHER--

--PETER PARKER, BOY HASBEEN.

AT LEAST, THAT'S WHAT JONAH JAMESON WILL SAY WHEN HE HEARS I HAVE--

NO PICTURES? NONE?

LET ME REFRESH YOUR MEMORY, PARKER; WE PAID YOUR WAY TO FLORIDA SO YOU COULD PHOTOGRAPH THE MAN-THING--

--NOT TO GIVE YOU A FREE VACATION!

JONAH, LISTEN--

NO, PARKER-- YOU LISTEN! I'VE HEARD ABOUT YOUR PROBLEMS, BUT I'M A BUSINESSMAN--NOT A PHILANTHROPIST!

YOU WANT TO GOOF OFF, THAT'S FINE-- BUT YOU DON'T DO IT ON MY TIME!

I'M GOING TO MAKE YOU PAY ME BACK FOR THIS FLORIDA FIASCO, PARKER--

--IF NECESSARY, OUT OF YOUR HIDE!

MARY JANE WATSON, I AM *SHOCKED!* I NEVER THOUGHT A YOUNG GIRL LIKE YOU WOULD LET HERSELF BE *PUSHED ASIDE* BY ANOTHER WOMAN!

WHY, IT'S SIMPLY *DISGRACEFUL!*

MOST PEOPLE ONLY HAVE *ONE CHANCE* AT LOVE, DEAR--

--AND YOU MUSTN'T-- *MUSTN'T*-- LET IT SLIP BY!

MY DARLING *BEN* ALMOST DIDN'T *PROPOSE* TO ME, YOU KNOW-- HE WAS SUCH A *SHY* MAN...

IF I'D LEFT THINGS TO *HIM,* I'D BE AN OLD MAID --AND NOT EVEN HAVE MY *MEMORIES.*

YOU'RE SAYING I SHOULDN'T LET PETER *GO,* MRS. PARKER?

I'M SAYING YOU SHOULD THINK ABOUT YOUR *FUTURE,* CHILD.

SOMETIMES A PERSON LETS THEIR *PRIDE* GET THE *BETTER* OF THEM, YOU KNOW--

OH, MY-- THERE'S *ANNA.*

BEEP

BEEP

PRIDE IS THE WORST THING IN THE *WORLD,* MARY JANE.

IT KEEPS PEOPLE *APART*--WHEN THEY NEED EACH OTHER THE *MOST.*

YEAH...

NY 1355

YEAH, I SEE WHERE YOU'RE *COMING FROM,* MRS. PARKER.

MAYBE I *HAVE* BEEN A LITTLE *HARD-HEADED.* MAYBE YOU'RE *RIGHT.*

Y'KNOW, LADY-- YOU'RE PRETTY *TOGETHER!*

WELL, MY GOODNESS-- AT *MY* AGE, I CERTAINLY HOPE SO!

INTERMISSION, FOLKS.

GO GET YOUR *POP-CORN* AND YOUR *COKES* AND WHEN YOU COME BACK, WE'LL START IN ON *ACT TWO:*

NAMELY-- *WEB-SWINGING TIME!*

123

127

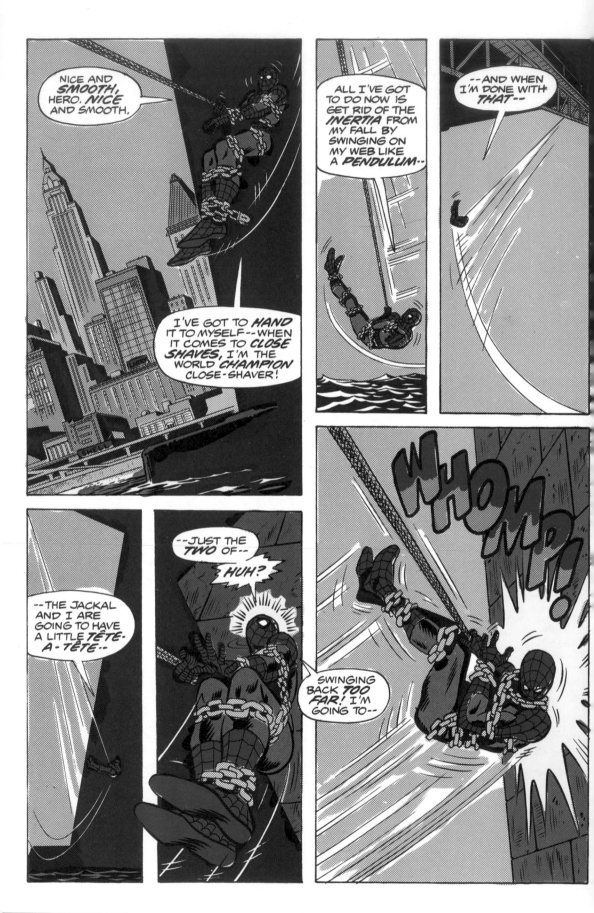

LIEUTENANT, I KNOW *EXACTLY* WHAT YOU MEAN!

LOOK AT *ME*: I HAD TO APPEAR *UNCONSCIOUS* SINCE YOU GUYS PICKED ME *UP*.

AND WHILE I HATE TO HAVE TO RAISE MY HAND *AGAINST* YOU--

--IT'S TIME I *GOT OFF*!

NO! YOU CAN'T *DO* THIS TO ME!

YOU *CAN'T*!

BRAKAKAKA

--AND I HOPE YOU BUY YOUR SHOES *WHOLESALE*, ARBUCKLE, *BECAUSE* YOU'LL BE POUNDING A *BEAT* FOR THE NEXT *TWENTY YEARS*!

STREET SCENE: ONE HALF HOUR *LATER*, ON MANHATTAN'S LOWER WEST SIDE...

WELL! IF IT ISN'T *PETER PARKER*-- THE LONELY GIRL'S FRIEND.

UH...HELLO, MARY JANE... *HEY*! THE MAN REMEMBERS MY *NAME*!

FOR A WHILE THERE, I'D THOUGHT YOU'D *FORGOTTEN* IT, FELLA-- OR AT LEAST MY *PHONE NUMBER*.

WHAT'S *WRONG*-- GWEN STACY TAKE UP ALL YOUR *FREE TIME* THESE DAYS, NOW THAT SHE'S *BACK*?*

UHH...

I'VE BEEN *THINKING* ABOUT THIS *GWEN STACY* THING, PETER--IN BETWEEN MY ASSIGNMENTS AT THE *DAILY BUGLE*-- AND I'VE GOT SOME *THOUGHTS* TO THROW AT YOU.

ONE: THE *REAL* GWEN-- THE GWEN *WE* KNOW IS *DEAD.*

SUCH AS?

TWO: THERE SEEMS TO BE A *SECOND* GWEN-- A *CLONE* OF THE FIRST.

THIS SECOND GWEN HAS ALL THE FIRST ONE'S MEMORIES-- BUT *HER* EXPERIENCE IS SEVERAL MONTHS OUT OF *DATE.*

GO ON!

YOU WANT MILK OR *CREAM*?

CREAM.

THREE: SOMEONE IS BEHIND THE APPEARANCE OF THIS SECOND GWEN-- SOMEONE WHO MEANS EITHER *YOU* OR *SPIDER-MAN* HARM.

I SAY THAT BECAUSE SPIDER-MAN WAS ORIGINALLY *BLAMED* FOR GWEN STACY'S *DEATH*--

--*BEFORE* IT WAS LEARNED THAT THE *GREEN GOBLIN* WAS RESPONSIBLE.

FOUR: WHOEVER HAS BROUGHT GWEN BACK *HAD* TO HAVE HAD ACCESS TO HER CELL TISSUE WHEN SHE WAS *ALIVE*--

THAT'S *IT*, NED--I THINK YOU'VE *GOT IT!*

TELL ME WHAT I'VE GOT.

GWEN AND I TOOK SEVERAL *CLASSES* TOGETHER AT COLLEGE--ONE OF THEM PROFESSOR WARREN'S *BIOLOGY CLASS!* I REMEMBER THE PROFESSOR'S *ASSISTANT* COLLECTING *CELL SAMPLES* FOR SOME PROJECT OR OTHER--

--SAMPLES FROM THE *ENTIRE CLASS*--

--*INCLUDING GWEN!*

IF PROFESSOR WARREN CAN REMEMBER WHAT *HAPPENED* TO THOSE SAMPLES--

LET'S *GO!*

UH--BUT BEFORE WE *DO*--MAYBE I'D BETTER PUT SOME *PANTS* ON--!

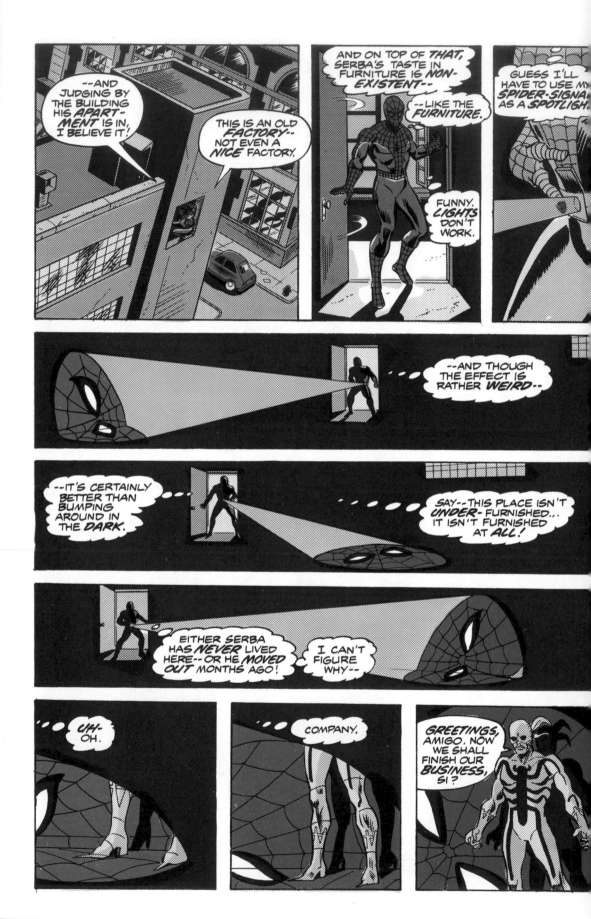

149

151

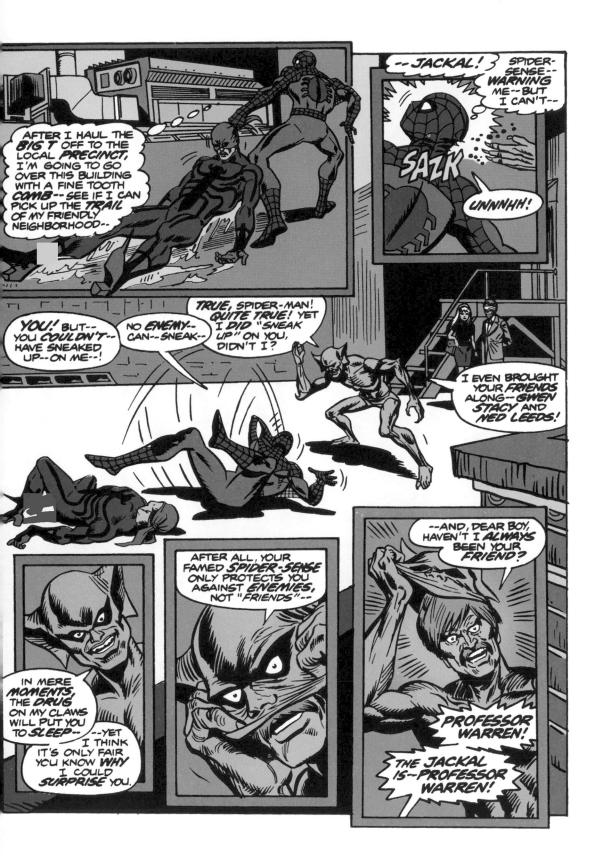

AFTER I HAUL THE *BIG T* OFF TO THE LOCAL *PRECINCT,* I'M GOING TO GO OVER THIS BUILDING WITH A FINE TOOTH *COMB*-- SEE IF I CAN PICK UP THE *TRAIL* OF MY FRIENDLY NEIGHBORHOOD--

--JACKAL! SPIDER-SENSE--WARNING ME--BUT I CAN'T--

SZIK

UNNNHH!

YOU! BUT-- YOU *COULDN'T*-- HAVE SNEAKED UP--ON ME--!

NO *ENEMY*-- CAN--SNEAK--

TRUE, SPIDER-MAN! QUITE TRUE! YET I *DID* "SNEAK UP" ON YOU, DIDN'T I?

I EVEN BROUGHT YOUR *FRIENDS* ALONG-- *GWEN STACY* AND *NED LEEDS!*

AFTER ALL, YOUR FAMED *SPIDER-SENSE* ONLY PROTECTS YOU AGAINST *ENEMIES,* NOT "FRIENDS"--

--AND, DEAR BOY, HAVEN'T I *ALWAYS* BEEN YOUR FRIEND?

IN MERE *MOMENTS,* THE *DRUG* ON MY CLAWS WILL PUT YOU TO *SLEEP*-- --YET I THINK IT'S ONLY FAIR YOU KNOW *WHY* I COULD *SURPRISE* YOU.

PROFESSOR WARREN!

THE JACKAL IS--PROFESSOR WARREN!

153

TIME, SPLINTERS AND SHARDS OF:

STRUCK FROM BEHIND BY THE JACKAL'S SPECIALLY *DRUGGED* CLAW, OUR HERO SLUMPS *FORWARD* ONTO THE TAR-PAPERED ROOF, HIS MIND ROAMING *BACKWARD* OVER THE PAST DAY'S EVENTS:

HE RECALLS BEING *THROWN* FROM THE TOP OF THE *BROOKLYN BRIDGE* BY THE JACKAL AND HIS TEMPORARY COHORT, *THE TARANTULA*--

POLICE

--AND HE RECALLS ESCAPING FROM THE POLICE BOAT WHICH *RESCUED* HIM AFTER HE'D INGENIOUSLY *BROKEN HIS FALL*--!

FURTHER, HE REMEMBERS GOING WITH *NED LEEDS* TO *PROFESSOR WARREN*, TO CHECK ON THE EXISTENCE OF CERTAIN *CELL SAMPLES* FROM WHICH GWEN STACY'S *CLONE* HAD BEEN CREATED--

--SAMPLES WHICH WARREN CLAIMED HAD BEEN *STOLEN* BY A MAN NAMED *ANTHONY SERBA.*

--AND THEN THE *CRUSHING* DEFEAT AT THE HANDS OF THE JACKAL STRIKING-- TYPICALLY-- FROM *BEHIND.*

YES, HE RELIVES IT *ALL:* THE FIGHT WITH *TARANTULA* ON THE ROOF OF SERBA'S OLD *APARTMENT*--

--THE *VICTORY*--

HE REMEMBERS, AND THEN THE MEMORY *COLLAPSES*--

THE NEXT SEVERAL MONTHS WERE QUITE *BUSY* ONES, PARKER. I HAD TO CARE FOR THE *CLONES*, RESIGN MY *JACKAL* EQUIPMENT AND COSTUME, TRAIN MYSELF *ATHLETICALLY*, ALL THE WHILE BEING DRIVEN BY ONE CONSUMING *PASSION*:

THE *RE-CREATION* OF A WOMAN I--THAT IS, A *GIRL* I FELT--I--

"THE *RE-CREATION* OF *GWEN STACY*--AND THE ACTING OUT OF MY *REVENGE* FOR HER SAVAGE *SLAYING!*

"AT LAST, THE DAY *CAME*--

"--HER CLONE CASKET OPENED WITH A PNEUMATIC *SIGH*--

--AND I FOUND MYSELF LOOKING AT *BEAUTY*, CHASTE AND PURE, UNSULLIED BY THE FILTH OF A WORLD GONE *MAD*.

"NATURALLY, SHE WAS COMPLETELY *INNOCENT*--

"--WITHOUT THE SLIGHTEST *MEMORY* OF HER LAST FEW HOURS OF *LIFE*.

"I *HELPED* HER FROM THE *CASKET*--

165

171

BLAST IT! ALL THIS *PACING* AND SOUL-SEARCHING IS ONLY HELPING TO WEAR OUT THE *FLOOR*.

VRAP!

I'VE GOTTA *DO* SOMETHING!

AND *THIS* TIME OF NIGHT, I'LL GET MORE DOIN' *DONE*... AS *SPIDER-MAN!*

KEEP *SAYING* IT, HERO... MAYBE YOU'LL START TO *BELIEVE* IT. AFTER ALL...

...*LOOK* WHAT YOU'VE ACCOMPLISHED--

"YOU PARTED *PERMANENTLY* WITH...

...THE *CLONED* VERSION OF GWEN STACY.

"AND YOU *HID* THE BODY OF YOUR *OTHER* SELF UNTIL YOU COULD BE *SURE* WHO'S THE *REAL* SPIDEY...!"

"YOU *DESTROYED* PROFESSOR WARREN'S *JACKAL* COSTUME SO NO ONE WILL KNOW HE *DIED* ANYTHING BUT A *HERO*.

--SINCE EVERYTHING WENT *BOOM* AT SHEA STADIUM LAST NIGHT. *

AND *THAT* YOU SHOULD BE ABLE TO LEARN RIGHT *HERE*...

...DR. *CURT* CONNERS' LABORATORY.

AT LAST!

MY *PATIENCE* SINCE ESCAPING PRISON IS FINALLY *REWARDED*.

I *KNEW* IF I MONITORED SITES *SPIDER-MAN* FREQUENTED REGULARLY IN THE PAST--

--HE'D EVENTUALLY FALL INTO MY *HANDS!*

WE WON'T ACCEPT *THAT* UNTIL *EVERY* TEST IS EXHAUSTED.

AND THERE'LL BE *PLENTY.* A CLONE IS GROWN FROM THE *CELL TISSUE* OF THE ORIGINAL PERSON... MAKING IT *APPEAR* TO BE AN *EXACT* DUPLICATE.

YET REALLY, IT'S A *NEWER* VERSION, DEVELOPED *FASTER,* THAT-- EVEN IF THE CLONE'S GIVEN THE SAME *MEMORY*-- MAKES FOR *DIFFERENCES. SUBTLE* ONES, ADMITTEDLY. PERHAPS PHYSIOLOGICAL, PERHAPS EMOTIONAL...

"...BUT *NOT* SO SUBTLE *WE* CAN'T FIND THEM!"

"STILL, TO BE *THOROUGH,* IT MUST BE A *LONG* SEARCH...

"...AND A *DEBILITATING* ONE."

BETTER LIE DOWN.

THOSE TESTS CAN MAKE EVEN *YOU* WOOZY...

...AND I WON'T HAVE THE *FINAL RESULTS* FOR SEVERAL MORE HOURS.

REST. IT COMES *HARD* TO SPIDEY... IT COMES *TROUBLED,* BUT COME IT *DOES*...

UNTIL...

W-WHA..? SOMEONE CALLING MY *NAME...?!*

COME OUT, SPIDER-MAN... I *KNOW* WHERE YOU ARE!

COME *OUT...* OR I COME IN *AFTER* YOU!

THE *VULTURE...?!* *NOW* OF ALL TIMES! CAN'T LET HIM *HARM* DOC CONNERS...

177

179

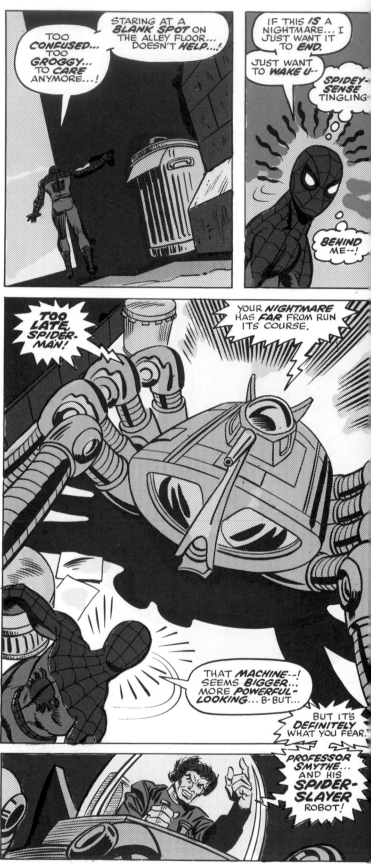

BUT *THIS* NIGHTMARE IS A *LIVING ONE*...!

WHUNG

THE SOUND IS A *MOIST* SOUND, A *TERRIBLE* SOUND. *FLESH* STRIKING WALLS OF BRICK AND STONE...

CREATED BY ME!

AND IT HAS ONLY JUST *BEGUN*...

MY VARIOUS *SPIDER-SLAYERS* WERE NEVER QUITE A *MATCH* FOR YOU...

...SO *THIS* TIME I GAVE THEM SOME *PRELIMINARY AID*...

...THREE *HUMANOID* ROBOTS.

WHUNG!

DESIGNED TO *LOOK* AND *REACT* LIKE *YOUR* FORMER FOES...

DESIGNED TO BATTER, TORMENT AND *EXHAUST* YOU PHYSICALLY...

THEN UPON SUFFICIENT IMPACT... *SELF-DESTRUCT!*

ACID CAPSULES WITHIN THEM ASSURED *TOTAL DISINTEGRATION*... SO THEY SEEMINGLY *VANISHED*...

...TO CONFUSE AND EXHAUST YOU *MENTALLY!*

LEAVING YOU ALL BUT *DEFENSELESS*...

...WHEN AT *LAST* MY SPIDER-SLAYER AND I *FACED* YOU...

WHUNG!

...THE *PERFECT VICTIM!*

TOO *WEAK*... TOO FAR *GONE*... TO *SNAP* TENTACLE...

H-HE'S...*REALLY*... GOT...ME...!

186

189

THINGS ARE SENT HERE TO *DIE*--TO BE *PURIFIED* BY *FIRE* AND REDUCED TO VAGRANT *ASH*-- OR BE PILED INTO *BARGES* AND UN-CEREMONIOUSLY *DUMPED* BEYOND THE 12-MILE LIMIT.

THE NEW YORK CITY DEPARTMENT OF SANITATION CALLS THIS PLACE AN *INCINERATING PLANT*; THE LOCAL RESIDENTS CALL IT AN *EYESORE*; BUT THE WEB-SLINGING *SPIDER-MAN* MAY WELL CALL IT A *GODSEND*--

--FOR HE HAS COME TO THESE JUTTING TOWERS DEEP IN THE WILDS OF BROOKLYN--*TO RID HIMSELF OF A NIGHTMARE!*